Weekly Reader Books presents

An Early I CAN READ Book

Ottie and the Star

by Laura Jean Allen

HARPER & ROW, PUBLISHERS

New York, Hagerstown, San Francisco, London

This book is a presentation of Weekly Reader Books.
Weekly Reader Books offers book clubs for children from
preschool through junior high school.

For further information write to:
Weekly Reader Books
1250 Fairwood Ave.
Columbus, Ohio 43216

Library of Congress Cataloging in Publication Data
Allen, Laura Jean.
    Ottie and the star.

    (An Early I can read book)
    SUMMARY: A little otter encounters a shark,
a dolphin, and a starfish while trying to catch a
star.
    [1. Otters—Fiction.   2. Marine animals—
Fiction]   I. Title.
PZ7. A42740t   [E]   78-22485
ISBN 0-06-020107-X
ISBN 0-06-020108-8 lib. bdg.

To Mirtsa with love

Ottie and his mother

lived by the sea.

One night Ottie asked,

"What are those, Mama?"

"Stars," said his mother.

"I want one," said Ottie.

"They are too far away,"

said his mother.

Ottie looked at some stars

in the water.

"They are *not* too far away,"

he said to himself.

"I will get one."

9

Ottie swam down,

down,

down,

looking for a star.

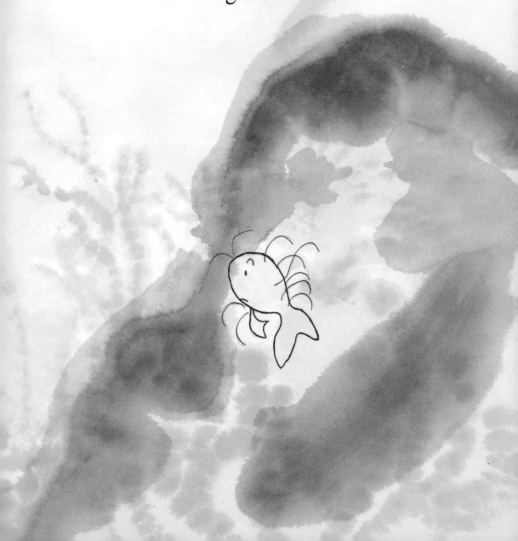

He saw something

shiny and sharp

behind a rock.

"A star!" Ottie shouted.

And he swam over to get it.

But it was a shark!

And it wanted to get Ottie.

Ottie swam fast.

He twisted and he turned.

But the shark was getting closer.

14

Just in time

Ottie saw a cave

and slipped into it.

Ottie waited a long time.

Then he looked outside.

"Hi," said a dolphin.

"A shark almost got me!" Ottie cried.

"Hop on my back," said the dolphin.

"You will be safe with me!"

Ottie and the dolphin

swam around

and around.

They swam over

and under

and up

and down.

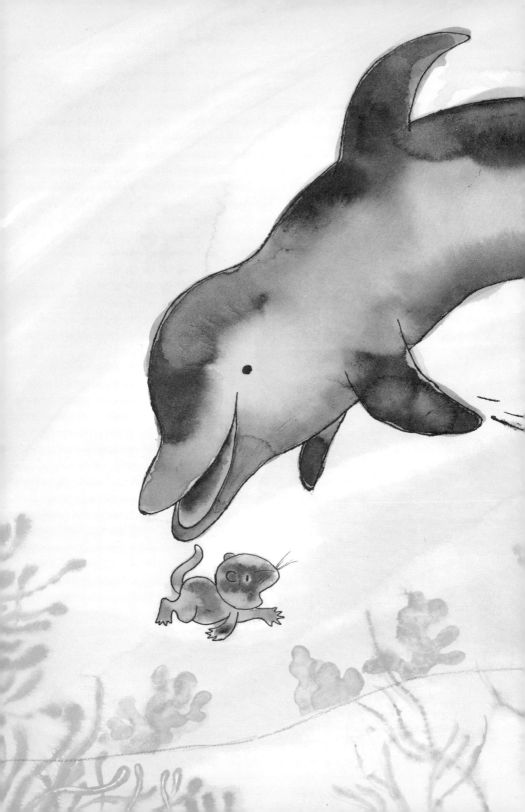

Ottie saw a star.

"I have to get off now!" he said.

"Thank you, Dolphin."

"You are welcome,"

said the dolphin.

Ottie swam down

and grabbed the star.

"Let go of me!" cried the star.

But Ottie held on to the star

and swam up,

up,

to the top of the water.

25

"Look, Mama!

I caught a star!"

"That is not a star, Ottie,"

said his mother.

"It is a star*fish*."

"But he looks like a star, Mama."

"So he does," said his mother.

"But stars are

up in the sky.

Starfish live

down in the water."

"And I want to go home!"

said the starfish.

"I'm sorry I scared you, Starfish,"

said Ottie.

"I'll take you home."

"I don't need your help!"

said Starfish.

"I can swim."

"Good-bye, Starfish," said Ottie.

"Good-bye, Ottie," called Starfish.

Ottie and his mother

watched Starfish

plop into the water.

31

"Someday," said Ottie,

"I will visit Starfish."

Then he told his mother

all about the shark

and the dolphin.

WIND AND
PEOPLE

NIKKI BUNDEY

 Carolrhoda Books, Inc. / Minneapolis

First American edition published in 2001 by
Carolrhoda Books, Inc.

All the words that appear in **bold** type are explained
in the glossary that starts on page 30.

John Hatt 4t / Juliet Highet 14t / Michael MacIntyre 22 / Hutchison Picture
Library; Alexis Wallerstein—title page / Alex Macnaughton 4b / Jeremy
Nicholl 5 / Ben Edwards 6 / Bruce Stephens 9b / Alan Keohane 23b / Impact
Photos; Rich Kirchner 12t / Jane Gifford 16t / T Kitchin & V Hurst 18 /
Kevin Schafer 25 / NHPA; Mike Kolloffel—cover (inset) right / Jorgen
Schytte 14b / Mark Edwards 15t,16b / E Duigenan-Christian Aid 15b / Tantyo
Bangun 27b / Still Pictures; 7b, 9t / The Stock Market; T Noorits—cover
(background) / C Webb—cover (inset) left / M Feeney 7t / H Rogers 8, 20,
27t, 29t / S Grant 10 / Aperture Photobank 11b / N Ray 12b / B Turner 13 / S
Grant / 17 / A Tovy 19 / T Fisher 21t / Richard Blosse 21b / P Barkham 23t /
D Brooker 24t / TH-Foto Werbung 24b / Chris Parker 26 / T Freeman 28 / J
Ellard 29b / 11t /TRIP.

Illustrations by Artistic License/Genny Haines, Tracy Fennell

Carolrhoda Books, Inc.
A division of Lerner Publishing Group
241 First Avenue North
Minneapolis, MN 55401 U.S.A.

Website address: www.lernerbooks.com

A ZOË BOOK

Copyright © 2000 Zoë Books Limited. Originally produced in 2000 by Zoë Books
Limited, Winchester, England

Library of Congress Cataloging-in-Publication Data

Bundey, Nikki, 1948–
     Wind and people / by Nikki Bundey
        p. cm. — (The science of weather)
     Includes index.
     Summary: Discusses how people cope with, use, and control wind, exploring its
effects on clothing, housing, and natural disasters.
        ISBN 1-57505-495-7 (lib. bdg. : alk. paper)
        1. Winds—Juvenile literature. 2. Weather—Juvenile literature. [1. Winds.]
     I. Title. II. Series: Bundey, Nikki, 1948– The science of weather.
     QC931.4.B83   2001
     551.51'8—dc21
                                                                              00-023716

Printed in Italy by Grafedit SpA
Bound in the United States of America
1 2 3 4 5 6—OS—06 05 04 03 02 01

CONTENTS

WHEN THE WIND BLOWS

The **wind** blows on your face. It tugs at your hair and clothes, but you cannot see it. What is it? Wind is a **current**, or moving stream, of air. When hot air rises, cooler air rushes in to take its place. This moving air is called wind.

Air is made up of a mixture of **gases**. They form the **atmosphere**, a layer around the earth. Beyond the atmosphere lies space.

These children in Bali, an island in Indonesia, are flying kites. The force of the wind blows the kites upward. Only the string keeps the kites from blowing away.

Although we cannot see the wind, we can feel it, and we can see what it does. The wind is blowing these clouds across the sky.

The force of the wind has blown this umbrella inside out. Wind affects our **weather**. It brings rain and snow and makes us feel hot or cold.

People, plants, and animals need the gases in the air for life. Humans breathe in **oxygen**, and plants give it out. Oxygen passes from our lungs into the blood that flows around our bodies. We breathe out **carbon dioxide**, which plants take in.

Air also contains a gas called **water vapor**. As it cools, water vapor turns into tiny water droplets, which hang in the air as clouds. The droplets gather together and fall as rain.

See for Yourself

- Take a deep breath of air. Breathe out again onto the surface of a small mirror.
- Droplets form on the mirror's surface. What are they made of?
- Which gas in the air produced them?

COOL OR WARM?

Winds can lower the **temperature** of the air and cool down the human body. We enjoy cool winds when we are feeling hot.

If the weather is already cold, winds can lower our body temperatures to dangerous levels. This effect is called **windchill**. For example, a 20-mile-per-hour wind can make a temperature of 32 degrees Fahrenheit feel like 5 degrees. Humans cannot survive in very low temperatures.

This palace in Jaipur, India, is more than 260 years old. Its windows are open screens that let winds blow through the rooms. Winds help keep people cool in hot places.

If there is no wind, we can make air currents by waving a fan or a sheet of paper. This Spanish woman holds a fan decorated with lace.

Birds and animals have feathers and fur to keep their bodies warm in cold winds. Humans have very little body hair, except on the tops of their heads. Like fur and feathers, hair prevents heat loss.

When the human body becomes too cold, it tries to protect itself. Tiny raised bumps, called goose bumps, form on the skin. Goose bumps raise tiny hairs that trap air around the body, providing **insulation** to keep us warm.

Winds that blow from a hot, dry region, such as a desert, are dry and warm. Hot winds can melt winter snows and warm us up.

CLOTHES AND FABRICS

Maybe you have seen laundry flap on the clothes line on a windy day. The wind helps turn the **liquid** water in the clothes into water vapor. This process is called **evaporation**.

The wind's drying power can be very useful. Wind can dry wet paint and make wet concrete harden. This power can be harmful, too. Wind sometimes dries out the natural moisture in human skin, causing it to crack.

Heavy jeans and thick sweaters can soak up a lot of water. They will take longer to dry than the thin, light, cotton clothes in the photograph.

After long exposure to the wind, human skin becomes red, chapped, and sore. Farmers and sailors need to protect their skin from the wind.

During the Stone Age, people wrapped themselves in furs and hides for protection from the wind. Modern people wear all sorts of clothing. It breaks the wind's force and stops its chilling and drying effect on our skin. Clothes provide insulation, allowing the body to keep in its heat and moisture.

Some fabrics are **windproof**. The tighter the weave, the better the fabrics keep warmth in and cold out. Looser weaves allow wind to pass through, keeping people cool in hot weather.

WIND AS A FORCE

What happens when the wind meets an object? A paper bag may blow away, but a heavier object, such as a trash can, may stand firm. Railings and fences allow the wind to pass through. The wind slips around the edges of rounded fence posts and rails.

The force with which objects block the wind is called **wind resistance**. The way objects behave as the wind flows around them is called **aerodynamics**.

These flags are light. They flutter and flap until the wind dies down.

People use computers to study the aerodynamic forces that affect vehicles on the road. Designers test models like this one, before making real cars.

Imagine you are designing a truck. You'll want to make the truck **streamlined,** so that it moves through the air without much wind resistance. Streamlining will keep the truck from overturning in a strong wind. The truck will also move faster and need less energy from gasoline.

Humans can make themselves streamlined, too. This ski jumper wears tight-fitting clothes that will not catch the wind and slow her down. She leans forward to reduce wind resistance.

SHELTER FROM THE WIND

The first humans may have gone inside caves to find shelter from the wind, sun, and rain. Later, people learned to make huts from tree branches and tents from animal hides.

We still use tents. Modern tents are made of light fabrics that catch the wind. Poles help support the sides of the tent. Ropes anchor the tent to the ground. **Foundations** are structures that anchor houses to the ground. Strong roofs protect houses from the wind.

Tents are anchored firmly to the ground. They have to withstand the wind's tugging force.

Mountaintops are exposed to strong winds. Houses in the mountains need heavy roofs as protection from the force of the wind.

A **weather vane** moves around as the wind changes direction. We name winds by the direction from which they blow. A northerly wind blows from the north.

Mountainsides and seashores can be very windy. Houses there need to be very strong. Most houses are built in sheltered places, such as valleys.

The **prevailing winds** are large belts of wind that circle the earth. In North America, prevailing winds blow from the west. Near the **equator**, winds blow from the east. Local winds affect smaller areas, such as mountainsides and coastlines.

See for Yourself

1. Cut out an arrowhead and a vane from cardboard, as shown.

2. Cut a slit in each end of a drinking straw. Attach the vane and the arrowhead, as shown.

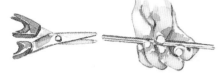

3. Push a thumbtack through the middle of the straw.

4. Stick the thumbtack into an eraser on a pencil. Anchor the pointed end of the pencil in a block of modeling clay. Stick the clay on top of an outdoor wall or fence.

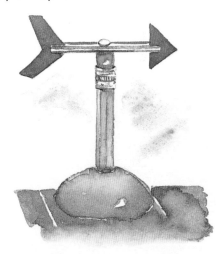

5. Use a compass to find north, south, east, and west and mark these directions on the clay.
6. The arrow will turn and point into the wind.
7. Record wind directions in a notebook.

FARMING IN THE WIND

Winds bring many problems for farmers. Strong winds sometimes blow soil away, leaving only dust and rock. This process is called **soil erosion**. Winds may carry desert sand, which covers soil and crops. Winds can also damage tender seedlings, buds, and fruit.

Farmers need windbreaks to anchor the soil and protect crops. Hedges or trees act as barriers against the force and chill of the wind.

By planting trees and grasses, people try to keep the Sahara Desert from spreading. Plants provide a barrier against dust storms, and their roots anchor the soil.

Strong winds can bring disaster. They can blow down crops such as wheat or corn before they are ready to be harvested.

The monsoon winds bring rain to Asia. Rain makes it possible to grow rice, millet, and corn. Millions of people depend on these crops for their daily food.

Some winds are very useful to farmers. They bring rain, which plants and animals need. The **monsoon** winds of southern Asia carry vast amounts of moisture from the Indian Ocean. During the monsoon season, heavy rains fall over the hot, dry lands of India, bringing much-needed water to the crops.

The wind helps farmers sort grain for use as food. As the grain is shaken, husks and other unwanted plant parts blow away. This process is called winnowing.

15

WIND IN THE FOREST

Strong winds such as **gales** and **hurricanes** often blow down trees. They rip out the roots that anchor the trees in the ground. Within a few years, new trees grow to take the place of the old ones.

All over the world, people are cutting down huge areas of forest. Without tree roots to hold the soil firmly in place, it will soon blow away. If no new trees are planted, the forests will disappear.

After a storm destroys trees, a forest usually grows back within ten or twenty years.

In the rain forests near the Amazon River, many trees have been cut down. Wind and rain have eroded the soil in many places. The land becomes useless.

Winds fan forest fires, and the fires spread rapidly over large areas. The oxygen in the air helps the blaze grow. Fires threaten human and animal life, as well as plants and houses. People often cut broad paths through the forest to stop fires from spreading. These gaps are called firebreaks.

Flames cannot leap across a broad gap where there are no trees to burn. If sparks do blow across a firebreak, new blazes can start.

WINDY CITIES

Strong winds can damage high buildings and other structures. Radio and television towers need support from strong steel cables. Bridges have to withstand heavy pounding by both wind and waves.

Before high structures are built, scientists test models. They measure the stresses that strong winds may cause. The tests take place in a **wind tunnel**. An electric fan blows air currents at the model, while **pressure sensors** record the effects of the wind.

In 1940 a strong wind shook the Tacoma Narrows Bridge in Washington State. The wind set off vibrations that made the bridge collapse.

Steel cables hold these towers in position. The cables are anchored deep in concrete beds.

In the United States, many cities have tall skyscrapers. The John Hancock Center in Chicago is 1,1 29 feet high. It has big Xs on its side called **cross braces**. ` They support the structure against the force of the wind.

Tall skyscrapers sway very slightly in high winds. This swaying helps to reduce the buildings' wind resistance. The buildings must not move too much, though, or they might fall down. They must be very strong.

Skyscrapers often create powerful air currents. Wind rushes between the tall buildings like water running through a funnel.

See for Yourself

- Make a tower from about twenty toy building bricks or blocks.
- Ask a grown-up to help you test the tower's strength by blowing at it with an electric hair dryer from various distances and angles.

- Try building single, double, and four-square towers. Brace the tower with rubber bands and rulers. Which type of tower is strongest?

SAILS AND WINGS

For thousands of years, people have used wind power to sail ships. The wind fills a ship's sails and pushes it forward. The prevailing winds around the equator are called trade winds. They once moved trading ships around the world. In some modern sailboats, computers control the angle of the sails as they catch the wind, helping the boats move more quickly.

The ship's sails stretch against the wind. It is the power of this wind resistance that moves the ship along. The bottom of the ship is streamlined to move smoothly through the sea.

This sailing craft is designed to race over land. Its power comes from the wind in its sails, but it moves on wheels. **Friction** helps the wheels grip the sand.

Air currents help airplanes stay aloft. Planes climb by taking off into the wind. A tailwind pushes the plane along.

Planes stay up in the sky because air rushing under the wings brings pressure from below, pushing the wings upward. To land, the pilot can extend flaps from the wings. The flaps increase wind resistance and slow the plane down. Pilots must check wind speed and direction before and during each flight.

A small aircraft takes off into the wind. A **wind sock** by the runway allows the pilot to check the wind direction.

WIND SPORTS

The wind blows sailboards and big boats called yachts over the waves. Oceans and large lakes are often windy.

Sea breezes blow during the day, when cool air over the water rushes toward the warmer land. At night, when the land cools down, the wind blows back toward the sea. In hot places, people often welcome the sea breeze on humid summer days. Sailors adjust their sails to catch the breeze.

The wind fills the sail attached to the sailboard. Gripping the bar, the windsurfer uses the weight of his or her body to balance the weight of the sail.

A hang glider has large wings made of tough, light fabric. People launch hang gliders from steep hillsides into rising air currents. Hang gliders have been known to drift in the air for nearly 310 miles.

Gliders, hang gliders, and hot-air balloons are crafts that fly without engines. They use rising currents of hot air, called thermals and updrafts, to stay up. Updrafts are common near hills and cliffs, where moving air is often forced upward. Birds also use rising air currents to gain height.

In 1999, a hot-air balloon traveled all the way around the world. It made use of fast, high-level westerly winds called **jet streams**.

WIND ENERGY

People have used the power of the wind to run machinery for more than 1,300 years. **Windmills** once turned heavy stones that ground wheat into flour. The windmills had huge sails that turned in the wind. As the sails whirled, they drove wheels, shafts, and gears. Some windmills were used to pump water. Modern windmills produce electricity.

Some windmills had a top that moved around with the wind. This rotating cap moved the windmill's sails, so that they always faced the wind and whirled around.

In the Netherlands, windmills like this one were once used to pump water out of marshland.

This wind farm is in California. The world's biggest wind turbine is in Hawaii. Its blades are more than 100 yards long.

The wind turbine is a modern type of windmill. Its **rotors,** or blades, spin around to **generate** electricity. Large groups of turbines are called wind farms. Wind energy is clean and safe. Fuels such as gas and coal can be used only once, but the wind never stops blowing for long. Wind is a **renewable energy** source.

See for Yourself

- Buy a hand-held toy windmill.
- Choose a windy site and stick the windmill in the soil.
- At which angle to the wind does the windmill spin most easily?
- Watching the windmill over a long time, can you figure out the direction of the prevailing wind?

DANGER IN THE WIND

Strong winds can damage buildings and spread fire across cities. They can blow down trees and roofs, killing or injuring people. They can drive waves inland from the ocean, flooding houses and fields. They can pile up snow into huge **drifts**, which block roads and railways. Sometimes bridges have to be closed in high winds, and ships may need to take shelter.

Strong winds can cause high waves and flooding. Large breakers crash against seawalls and waterfronts. Their impact is powerful and can be very destructive.

The stone of this ancient building has been damaged by air pollution. Some buildings have to be cleaned regularly because of pollution in the air.

Winds often carry dust and sand over long distances. They may spread poisonous gases from factories, smoke from chimneys and fires, or exhaust fumes from cars and trucks. Winds can also spread deadly **radioactive** dust from **nuclear power** stations. These substances **pollute** the earth, poisoning farmland and making people sick.

Winds may carry water vapor that contains pollution from factories. The water vapor falls as **acid rain**, which poisons forests, lakes, and rivers. People must work hard to prevent air pollution.

Winds carried the smoke from forest fires and pollution over a wide area of Indonesia in 1997.

WIND SCIENCE

Wind helps us in many ways, but it can harm us, too. Scientists study the wind so that they can **forecast** weather conditions. People who study the weather are called **meteorologists**.

They use instruments to measure weather conditions. **Anemometers** measure wind speed. **Barometers** measure the force of the atmosphere pressing down on the earth's surface.

This anemometer has cups that whirl around in the wind. It sends information about wind speeds to traffic control centers, which warn drivers about dangerous weather conditions.

A barometer records air pressure. The information it provides helps meteorologists forecast wind direction and force. At home, people use barometers to help forecast the weather.

Large areas of low **air pressure** bring rainy, gloomy weather conditions. Areas of high pressure bring dry, clear weather. As weather systems move through the sky, they spin around. Winds swirl around high- and low-pressure systems in opposite directions. In northern areas, the systems spin clockwise. In southern areas, they spin counter-clockwise.

Satellites track weather systems as they travel around the earth. The information collected by satellites helps meteorologists make weather maps.

GLOSSARY

acid rain Rain polluted by chemicals in the air

aerodynamics The effects of air on objects in motion

air pressure The force with which the atmosphere presses on the ground

anemometer Any instrument used to measure wind speed

atmosphere The layer of gases around a planet

barometer An instrument that measures air pressure

carbon dioxide A gas in the earth's atmosphere

cross braces Beams that help strengthen a building

current A movement of air or water

drift Snow piled up in a great heap by the wind

equator An imaginary line drawn around the middle of the earth

evaporate To change from a liquid into a gas

forecast To predict future weather conditions

foundations Underground structures that anchor buildings to the ground

friction The force that slows one object as it rubs against another

gale A strong wind measuring 39 to 54 miles per hour

gas An airy substance that fills any space in which it is contained

generate To produce something, such as electricity

hurricane A tropical storm with winds measuring more than 74 miles per hour

insulation A barrier that prevents the transfer of heat

jet streams Extremely fast, high winds that move around the earth

liquid A fluid substance, such as water

meteorologists Scientists who study the weather

monsoon Seasonal, rain-bearing winds in southern Asia

nuclear power Energy made by changing the structure of atoms

oxygen A life-giving gas found in air and water

pollute To poison air, land, or water

pressure sensor An instrument used to measure the effects of airflow

prevailing winds The winds most commonly found in a region

radioactive Containing a dangerous type of energy

renewable energy Power that can be used over and over again

rotor A spinning blade, found on a wind turbine or other machine

satellite	A spacecraft that circles a planet
sea breeze	A cool breeze blowing from water toward the land
soil erosion	The loss of soil by the action of wind or rain
streamlined	Designed to reduce wind resistance
temperature	Warmth or cold, measured in degrees
water vapor	A gas created when water evaporates
weather	Atmospheric conditions sich as wind, rain, and clouds
weather vane	A device that spins to show the direction of the wind
wind	A movement of air
windchill	The cooling effect of wind combined with a low temperature
windmill	A building with large sails that turn in the wind and run machinery
windproof	Preventing the passage of wind
wind resistance	The force with which objects withstand the wind
wind sock	A cloth tube designed to catch the wind, showing its direction and force
wind tunnel	A chamber used to test the way in which air flows around an object

INDEX